THE FUNNY FIXES
of the Floogle Family

the Funny Fixes of the
FLOOGLE FAMILY

Story by GERTRUDE CRAMPTON

Illustrated by Dorothy Maas

j

THE BOBBS-MERRILL COMPANY, INC.
Publishers
INDIANAPOLIS   NEW YORK

CONTENTS

PAGE

THE FUNNY FIXES
of the Floogle Family

1: The Floogles Have Their Picture Taken

The Floogles are very nice people—Mr. Floogle and Mrs. Floogle and Amos Floogle and Fanny Flora Floogle and their dog, Snitkin Floogle. Everybody likes the Floogles. If only the Floogles weren't always getting so *confused*. Like the time the photographer came to their house.

He was a very old photographer, and his camera was as heavy as it was old. And when he saw Mr. Floogle cheerfully raking the grass the old man called across the fence.

"Sir! I am old and tired. The road is dusty and the camera heavy. May I have a drink of water before I go into the town?"

"Come in! Come in!" cried Mr. Floogle.

And Mrs. Floogle sniffed. "Water, indeed! Bring him into my kitchen for a glass of cold milk."

So there was a flurry and a scurry while Amos sliced ham for a sandwich—and cut his finger, of course—and Fanny Flora got a plate of fresh-baked cookies and Mr. Floogle cut the cheese and Mrs. Floogle poured the cold milk and Snitkin sat up and begged.

"Well," said the old man. "Well!"

And when he'd finished his fine lunch he eased his belt a comfortable notch and said, "Now I will do what kindness I can for you. I will take your picture. A fine family picture of all of you."

The Floogles were as excited as bluejays.

It would be wonderful. It would be splendid. It would be a great treat. They would send the picture to Aunt Hepzibah Floogle—no, to Cousin Ermintrude Floogle—perhaps to Big

Grandfather Floogle. Well, that could be decided later.

And all the while the old photographer grew sleepier and sleepier, for the day was warm, the lunch had been good and the photographer was older than his camera.

"Come along, now," said Mrs. Floogle. "It's time we had our picture taken."

So the old man arranged the Floogles carefully, with Snitkin in front since he was the smallest. Then the old photographer pulled the black cloth over his head and was ready.

But Mr. Floogle said, "Oh, this will not do! Fanny Flora should be in front, for Aunt Hepzibah will want to see how nicely her curls swing."

So Fanny Flora stood in front, and Snitkin sat beside her.

Then the old photographer pulled the black cloth over his head and was ready.

But Mrs. Floogle said, "Oh, this will not do,

either. Amos must be in front, too. Big Grand-father will want to see how straight his front teeth grew in."

So Amos stood in front, too, and Snitkin was in the middle.

Then the old photographer pulled the black cloth over his head and was ready.

But Fanny Flora said, "This will not do. Cousin Ermintrude will want to see Mama's beautiful new dress with the morning glories, and yellow buttons all the way to the hem."

And by this time the old photographer was so sleepy that he could not keep even one eye open.

"I'll just rest a minute," he said, "while you make up your minds." He sank into Mr. Floo-gle's own comfortable chair and at once was snoring gently and politely.

At last the Floogles made up their minds.

Everybody was to stand in front so that all the relatives could see how nicely Fanny Flora's curls swung, how straight Amos' front teeth had grown in, how beautiful Mrs. Floogle's morning-glory dress was and how magnificently Mr. Floogle's gold watch chain looped across his vest.

"But it is too bad to wake the old man," said Mrs. Floogle. "He seems so tired."

"We needn't call him," said Amos Floogle, who had once found a broken Brownie and consequently knew all about cameras. "You take the picture by pinching the little bulb on that cord. And I think the cord is long enough so that I can stand in the picture and still pinch the little bulb."

And it was.

"Now I'll peek under the black cloth," said Amos, "and see what our picture looks like before I pinch the bulb."

So Amos Floogle peeked under the black cloth.

"My goodness!" he cried. "This is terrible. We are upside down!"

"Let me see," said Mr. Floogle. So he peeked under the black cloth.

"We are indeed upside down," said Mr. Floogle gravely.

"Oh, dear!" said Mrs. Floogle. "I don't mind so much for myself. I've lived a long time without a picture, and I can live longer if need be.

"But the old photographer was trying so hard to be nice. It is a sad thing to disappoint him. We must do something."

So the Floogles thought and thought—in their confused way of thinking.

"If the old camera takes pictures upside down . . . " said Mr. Floogle.

"And we want our picture right side up . . ." said Amos Floogle.

"Then we must . . . " said Fanny Flora Floogle.

"If Fanny Flora and I want our faces to show clear, we must . . ." said Mrs. Floogle.

"Of course," said Amos Floogle.

"Naturally," said Mr. Floogle.

"And Snitkin?" asked Fanny Flora.

"Snitkin cannot be in this picture, I'm afraid," decided Mr. Floogle.

So the Floogles got ready.

And Amos Floogle said "Hup!" for practice and peeked under the black cloth.

"As right as rain," he said and took his place in the picture, the long cord and the little bulb handy.

"One, two, three, hup!" said Mr. Floogle, and Amos pinched the little bulb.

"There!" said all the Floogles happily.

The shadows were long and the robins noisy when the old photographer woke from his dreaming.

"Your picture!" he cried.

But the Floogles gave him supper and told him not to worry, for they'd taken the picture themselves.

So the old man went to the barn and developed

the picture. And he was so puzzled with the picture he got that the Floogles had to explain what they had done.

"But the people *always* look upside down in a camera like this one," the photographer said.

When the old man had wiped the laughter tears from his eyes, he took a proper picture of the Floogles and promised to make enough copies for Aunt Hepzibah and Cousin Ermintrude and Big Grandfather and Little Grandmother. And he did.

But the Floogles like better the picture they took while the old man was sleeping. So they keep it on top of the piano with a lace doily under it.

Their friends look at it and look at it, for it is a very unusual picture.

"Hold it so that the Floogles are standing," say their friends, "and the table and chairs all hang from the ceiling.

"Hold it so that the tables and chair are on

the floor properly and the Floogles are hanging by their toes. It is *very* confusing."

And it is. For the Floogles have promised one another they will never, *never, NEVER* tell they were so confused that they stood on their heads to take their own picture.

2: The Floogles
Go to the Railroad Station

Everyone likes the Floogles. Everyone likes *all* the Floogles, for the Floogles are always polite and charming. Even Snitkin Floogle is polite and barks no louder than need be when chasing a cat. If only the Floogles were not just as confused as they are polite! Like the time Aunt Hepzibah was coming to visit.

"How wonderful!" cried Mrs. Floogle when she'd read Aunt Hepzibah's letter.

And Amos and Fanny Flora cried, "How wonderful!" too. For Aunt Hepzibah was a sensible person who never patted their heads and said how *much* they had grown. Instead, she

20

gave them a large box of candy and told them not to ruin their suppers.

So Amos and Fanny Flora were helpful as could be to their mother. They carried out comforters to hang on the line and aired the mattresses and polished the silver and made a full mess of the house, which, as anyone knows, is the way to get ready for company.

Even Snitkin was helpful, for he dug up all his old bones to give Aunt Hepzibah her choice.

And only Mr. Floogle did not bustle and rustle about cheerfully. He sat in his own comfortable chair and sucked on his pipe gloomily and had nothing at all to say for himself.

Mrs. Floogle was worried. "Aunt Hepzibah is very nice," she remarked.

"Very nice," Mr. Floogle agreed.

"I like Aunt Hepzibah," said Fanny Flora.

"So do I," said Mr. Floogle.

"She is fun," said Amos.

"Lots of fun," Mr. Floogle said.

"Well, then," asked Mrs. Floogle, not a little impatient, "why do you sit in your comfortable chair and suck on your pipe?"

"Don't you realize that we are going to be very impolite to Aunt Hepzibah?" asked Mr. Floogle. "Very impolite indeed."

"Oh, *no!*" cried Mrs. Floogle. "Not to Aunt Hepzibah! How?"

"Aunt Hepzibah will come on the train," explained Mr. Floogle, "and we will all be waiting at the station, even Snitkin."

"Surely that is polite," said Mrs. Floogle.

"Aunt Hepzibah will get off the train," said Mr. Floogle. "She will have a hatbox and four suitcases, the large box of candy for Amos and Fanny Flora, a rubber bone for Snitkin, a bundle of quilt blocks, her biggest pocketbook, and the basket she packs chicken sandwiches in to eat on the train.

"*And,*" went on Mr. Floogle gloomily, "we have *nothing* for Aunt Hepzibah and her hat-

box and her four suitcases and the large box of candy and Snitkin's rubber bone and her bundle of quilt blocks and her biggest pocketbook and her chicken-sandwich basket to ride home in.

"There we will be. There Aunt Hepzibah will be. And there will be the hatbox, the four suitcases, the large box of candy, the rubber bone, the bundle of quilt blocks, the biggest pocketbook and the chicken-sandwich basket. And nothing at all for driving her home in style and politeness."

"Oh, my!" said Mrs. Floogle. "I never thought of that."

Then Mrs. Floogle and Fanny Flora and Amos were as gloomy as Mr. Floogle had been, and Mr. Floogle was gloomier than ever.

"How about the wheelbarrow?" asked Amos at supper.

"Not very polite," said Mr. Floogle.

"Not very pretty," said Fanny Flora.

"Not very comfortable," said Mrs. Floogle.

"Oh," said Amos.

"How about my doll buggy?" asked Fanny Flora at breakfast.

"Not very polite," said Mr. Floogle.

"Not very large," said Amos.

"Not very comfortable," said Mrs. Floogle.

"Oh," said Fanny Flora.

"How about that old carriage that is tucked away in the barn?" asked Mrs. Floogle at lunch.

"Very polite," said Amos.

"Very comfortable," said Fanny Flora.

"Very large," said Mrs. Floogle.

"No horse," said Mr. Floogle.

"Oh," said Mrs. Floogle. "But—?"

"Certainly," said Amos, looking at Mr. Floogle.

"Of course," said Mr. Floogle.

And all the Floogles stopped being gloomy at once and went back to airing the mattresses and polishing the silver . . . all except Mr. Floogle. He got on the train and went to the city. And when he came back he carried a large box that was filled to bursting.

"We must start practicing at once," said Mr. Floogle as he opened the box. "I will be the front so that I can see where we are going, for the traffic is heavy at the station. Amos will be the back, and he must remember to stay bent over."

So Amos and Mr. Floogle tried on their costume.

"How do we look?" asked Mr. Floogle.

"Very good," said Mrs. Floogle. "A little large in front. A little small in back. But no one will notice."

"You will look better with a hat," said Fanny Flora. So she got Mr. Floogle's old straw hat, and they *did* look better.

"Watch us trot," said Mr. Floogle.

But he trotted one way, and Amos the other, and they did not look very good at all.

"We must practice," said Amos.

And so every night and every morning Mr. Floogle and Amos practiced behind the barn, for they wanted no one of their neighbors to know they were learning to be a horse.

At last it was the day when Aunt Hepzibah was coming, and everything was ready.

The house shone from one end to the other, and the roast of beef was ready for the oven.

Three pies waited on the pantry shelf, and there was a chocolate cake for nibbling on.

The old carriage was cleaned and waxed and polished, and its red wheels twinkled when they spun.

The harness was oiled, and the brass shone like gold.

And Mr. Floogle and Amos could walk and trot and gallop and canter.

And everyone was as happy as a lark when Amos and Mr. Floogle backed between the shafts, for now there was a polite way, and a comfortable way and a stylish way to bring home

Aunt Hepzibah and her hatbox and four suit-cases, the large box of candy for Amos and Fanny Flora, the rubber bone for Snitkin, the bundle of quilt blocks, the biggest pocketbook and the chicken-sandwich basket.

"Here we go," said Mrs. Floogle when she and Fanny Flora and Snitkin were nicely ar-ranged in the carriage.

She picked up the reins and straightened the whip she had faithfully promised not to use and said, "Giddap," in a loud, clear voice. And away went the Floogles to meet Aunt Hepzi-bah politely.

And if the Floogles had not been so, so polite, things might have worked out very well indeed.

Mr. Floogle and Amos trotted up to the station with a flourish. And everything was going fine.

Aunt Hepzibah's train puffed into the sta-tion with a flourish. And everything was going fine.

Aunt Hepzibah got off the train with a flourish, and also with her hatbox and four suitcases, the large box of candy, the rubber bone, the bundle of quilt blocks, the biggest pocketbook and the chicken-sandwich basket. And everything was going fine.

Mrs. Floogle spied the Mayor and the Mayor's wife, who had come to the station to meet the Mayor's grandmother. Mrs. Floogle smiled politely. Fanny Flora, after a poke from Mrs. Floogle, stood up in the carriage and curtsied neatly—which was quite a trick in a jouncy carriage. And everything was going fine.

But just then Mr. Floogle saw the Mayor and the Mayor's wife. "Remember your manners," he whispered to Amos.

But Mr. Floogle forgot he was being a horse. So he bowed politely and tipped his hat charmingly and poked Amos to remind him to bow politely, too. This did very queer things to the horse.

The Mayor stared.

The Mayor's wife screamed.

The Mayor's grandmother fainted.

The train snorted.

Other horses snapped their traces and jumped out of their shafts.

Four trucks had flat tires, and somebody blew the fire siren.

Aunt Hepzibah was so astonished that she dropped her hatbox and her four suitcases, the box of candy, the rubber bone, the bundle of quilt blocks, her pocketbook and the chicken-sandwich basket.

And a policeman gave the Floogle horse a ticket.

"What for?" demanded Mr. Floogle. This made the policeman almost swallow his whistle.

The policeman scratched his head, while Aunt Hepzibah got comfortably settled in the carriage. Mrs. Floogle picked up the reins to drive her comfortably and politely home in style.

"Yes, what for?" asked Aunt Hepzibah.

"Well . . . for being polite," the policeman said at last. And he wrote that on the ticket.

"For being polite?" Amos said. "Everyone should be polite."

"NOT HORSES!" shouted the policeman.

So that afternoon Mr. Floogle and Amos had to go to court for being polite. But everyone in the town went also and said they'd never had a gayer time at the station. So the Judge said he would not scold and he would not lecture and he would not punish Mr. Floogle and Amos if they would promise never to be a polite horse again.

Mr. Floogle promised that he and Amos would never even be a horse, let alone a polite horse.

"It makes my knees ache to trot," explained Mr. Floogle.

"It makes my back ache, no matter what we do," explained Amos.

So they all went home and ate the chicken

sandwiches Aunt Hepzibah had left in the basket, and the three pies and the chocolate cake. And Aunt Hepzibah said the next time she came to visit with her hatbox and four suitcases, the large box of candy, the rubber bone, the bundle of quilt blocks, the biggest pocketbook and the chicken-sandwich basket, Mr. Floogle could hire a taxi to bring her home comfortably and politely.

"Now, why didn't I think of that?" said Mr. Floogle.

3: The Floogles and Their Orchestra

Mr. Floogle has always loved music. "Give me a good waltz any day," says Mr. Floogle. "Or a polka. Or a jig." And he hums a gay tune—which *could* be a waltz, or a polka, or a jig. Mr. Floogle is not very certain in his humming.

"Give us music, too," agree Mrs. Floogle and Amos Floogle and Fanny Flora Floogle. Not Snitkin Floogle, though. Music hurts his ears.

And so one day Mr. Floogle decided it was high time *something* was done about music.

"Especially," said Mr. Floogle, "since there

is to be a fine dance in the new Fire Station. And no orchestra to play."

Mr. Floogle drew an imaginary bow across imaginary strings of an imaginary violin and said *he* would play the violin. He felt there wasn't anything particularly difficult about playing a violin.

Amos immediately decided he would play the cornet. It would be handy when he became a Boy Scout and blew a bugle. "Ta-tah-tee-ta-tah-tee!" Amos blew Taps.

"Better stick to cornet practice," advised Mr. Floogle.

And Amos said he would. At least until after the dance.

Fanny Flora said *she* thought nothing was prettier than playing the harp. Especially with her hair rolled up in fresh curls and a new dress to wear.

And Mrs. Floogle said it was a shame the boy down the road had cut the piano strings with his new knife on his last visit. Everyone knew an orchestra needed a piano, and besides, she had always intended to learn to play.

"Very simple," Mr. Floogle promised. "Amos and I will tie the strings together again."

So Mrs. Floogle was happy and rummaged through two old trunks in the attic for a little waltz, polka and jig music.

By the time she had it located, Mr. Floogle and Amos had the piano strings tied, and very neatly, too, with quite small knots. And the Floogles were ready for their first practice.

"One-a, two-a, three-and-four!" counted Mr. Floogle. Being the oldest, Mr. Floogle was the leader, of course.

The Floogles started bravely.

"Well," asked Mr. Floogle at the end, "how did we sound?"

But Mrs. Floogle admitted she had been so busy choosing white keys and black keys that she hadn't listened.

"Once more, then," said the leader.

The Floogle orchestra played again.

"Well?" asked Mr. Floogle.

"Well," said Mrs. Floogle, "I wasn't *quite* sure whether we played a jig or a polka or a waltz. And, of course, that is an important question for dancing."

"Well, yes," said Mr. Floogle.

"Besides," said Amos, "the piano was *much* too loud. I could not hear the violin. I could not hear anything except the black keys and the white keys."

"And the knots," added Fanny Flora.

"True," said Mr. Floogle.

And Mrs. Floogle looked hurt.

"Oh, well," said Mr. Floogle, "we will do better next time. Who can make an orchestra in one practice?"

So all the Floogles cheered up immensely. Even Snitkin, who had got far under Amos' bed and covered his ears with his paws.

Mrs. Floogle promised not to thump so hard at the next practice and hurried off to bake a pie to build up everyone's strength.

Mr. Floogle strolled down to the Fire Station to help watch the Fire Chief play checkers and to offer, very grandly, to have his orchestra play for the dance.

"The Fire Chief is extremely grateful," Mr. Floogle reported to Mrs. Floogle and Amos and Fanny Flora at supper. "And why not? Think how troublesome the Chief would find it, to be giving a dance in the new Fire Station, with no orchestra to play for the dancing."

"Think how troublesome *we* will find it," said Mrs. Floogle, "if our orchestra does not play nicely. And the dance in three days."

So the minute the supper dishes were washed and wiped dry on most of the edges, the Floogles had another practice.

"One-a, two-a, three-and-four," counted the leader.

"A very nice jig," said Mrs. Floogle at the end.

Mr. Floogle frowned. *"That* was a polka."

"Oh, dear!" said Mrs. Floogle.

"Oh, dear!" Snitkin howled under the bed.

"One-a, two-a, three-and-four," counted the leader.

Again and again and again.

But always the piano sounded too loud.

"No one can hear the harp," Fanny Flora complained.

"If you did not play so loudly," Amos pointed out to Mrs. Floogle, "no one could tell when you get confused with black keys and white."

Mrs. Floogle said she was doing her very best not to play so loudly.

"But after all," said Mrs. Floogle, "when I hit a black key it plays a black note. And there's nothing I can do about the matter."

She was so near tears that Amos immediately

ran to the drugstore and brought home a quart and a half of chocolate ice cream.

And Fanny Flora said it might well be her own fault about the harp. Perhaps she could hear it if she pinned up her curls for the next practice.

So Mrs. Floogle moved further and further away from tears and was quite cheerful by bed-time.

Early the next day the orchestra practiced again. One-a, two-a, three-and-four.

"Too loud!" said Mr. Floogle, still talking about the piano. "One-a, two-a, three-and-four! Again."

"Too loud," said Amos, still talking about the piano.

"Much too loud," growled Snitkin, talking about everything.

Mrs. Floogle was not near to tears. Nowhere near. She poked out her chin, and her lips made a straight line.

"*I'm* not too loud," said Mrs. Floogle. "*You're* too soft."

"Quite possible," agreed Mr. Floogle and Amos and Fanny Flora. "We'll try to play louder."

"Oh, *no!*" groaned Snitkin to himself.

The Floogles tried again.

One-a, two-a, three-and-four.

Everyone looked discouraged, and Snitkin's tail hung low.

"Maybe we will feel better after lunch and a short nap," said Fanny Flora.

So the orchestra had lunch and a short nap.

"Now then," said Mr. Floogle. "Here we go. Everyone loud . . . except the piano."

Mrs. Floogle tried hard not to touch the piano hard. Her hands were white doves in the shining sun. Her fingers were whispers on the black keys and the white keys. Her two feet were three feet away from the pedals.

"Too loud!" said the Floogles.

All except Mrs. Floogle. *She* said, "Too soft!" and was very determined about it. Even when Mr. Floogle and Amos and Fanny Flora said, "Too loud!" all over again.

Before the practicing was done, all the Floogles were feeling very hot and very tired and very cross. No one had a kind word for anyone, or even a pat for Snitkin.

At last Mr. Floogle lighted his pipe and looked at his family.

"Here, now," he said sorrowfully, "this will not do at all, and you know it.

"Floogles can be wrong.

"Floogles can be confused.

"But Floogles are never against one another."

"How true!" cried Mrs. Floogle.

"How right!" cried Amos.

"How clever!" cried Fanny Flora.

And all the Floogles smiled and said they'd been silly to be cross. They felt better immediately.

"But the fact remains," said Mrs. Floogle bravely, "that I am playing too loudly."

"Oh, no!" cried Mr. Floogle and Amos and Fanny Flora. "We are playing too softly."

So they tried again, full of good will and cheerful hearts and loving thoughts—but the piano was still too loud.

Mr. Floogle sighed. "We just do not make an orchestra."

Amos sighed. "And the dance in the new Fire Station tomorrow."

Fanny Flora sighed. "And my new dress ready, and the hem sewed in all the way around."

Mr. Floogle sighed. "And me so grand in my boasting and bragging about our orchestra. If only I had not promised!"

And gloom and darkness and silence and sorrow lived with the Floogles.

"But promise you did!" said Mrs. Floogle. "And promises made are promises to keep. So the Floogles must be an orchestra."

"Easy to say," said Mr. Floogle.

"Hard to do," said Amos.

"How?" asked Fanny Flora.

"We need help," Mrs. Floogle said firmly. And she pinned on her hat and buttoned up her coat and she went to the railroad station to find her Fifth Cousin Jasper.

Fifth Cousin Jasper was the brakeman and was busy indeed looking at brakes. But he listened carefully to Mrs. Floogle.

And when she had finished, he scratched his hair and shook his head. He said that, not being able himself to play the violin or the harp or the piano, he did not see how he'd be much help. But he obligingly agreed to do what he could. So he left his brakes and borrowed a car to drive Mrs. Floogle home.

Fifth Cousin Jasper sat in Mr. Floogle's comfortable chair, and the orchestra got ready.

"One-a, two-a, three-and-four," counted the leader. Away they went with a prancing jig.

When it was over, Mrs. Floogle said sadly, "I was too loud."

The others said sadly. "We were too soft."

Then they waited for Fifth Cousin Jasper to say something.

"I could hear the black keys and the white keys," said Fifth Cousin Jasper at last. "I could hear the knots. But I could not hear the violin or the cornet or the harp."

The Floogles groaned.

"And," said Fifth Cousin Jasper, "I *think* the reason I could not hear them is because there aren't any."

The Floogles looked at one another. The Floogles looked at their orchestra.

"I was so busy boasting and bragging and leading," said Mr. Floogle, "that I forgot about getting a violin."

"I was so busy planning to blow the Boy Scout bugle," said Amos, "that I forgot about getting a cornet."

"I was so busy pinning my hair in fresh curls," said Fanny Flora, "that I forgot about getting a harp."

"No wonder at all the piano was *always* louder than the violin and the harp and the cornet," said Mrs. Floogle.

"I could have told them that," said Snitkin to

himself. "A piano that's there always sounds louder than a violin or a cornet or a harp that isn't."

And all the Floogles looked terribly ashamed at being so confused.

"Oh, well," said Mr. Floogle at last.

Fifth Cousin Jasper began to laugh, and Mr. Floogle joined in, and Mrs. Floogle and Amos and Fanny Flora, until there was a whole orchestra of laughing. The cups danced in time in the cupboards, and Snitkin chased his tail.

"Oh, my!" Mrs. Floogle wiped the laughter tears out of her eyes. "Now what? The dance will be tomorrow night."

"Very simple," said Fifth Cousin Jasper. "My train goes to the city as soon as my brakes are repaired. I will get a harp and a violin and a cornet for you."

"Splendid!" Mr. Floogle cried.

"Excellent!" Fanny Flora cried.

"Wonderful!" Amos cried.

"Grrr!" Snitkin warned Fifth Cousin Jasper.

"You *can* play a violin and a harp and a cornet, can't you?" asked Fifth Cousin Jasper.

"Well, no!" said Mr. Floogle.

"Not exactly," said Amos.

"Only because we've never tried," said Fanny Flora.

"Oh, my! We're right back where we started," said Mrs. Floogle.

"Perhaps not," comforted Fifth Cousin Jasper. "Isn't there anything you *can* play?"

"A comb," said Mr. Floogle. "If it has tissue paper over it."

"A mouth organ," said Fanny Flora. "If it's not too big."

"A slide whistle," said Amos. "If the song doesn't slide too far."

"Now we're getting somewhere," said Fifth Cousin Jasper. "I happen to be an elegant sweet-potato man myself."

So Fifth Cousin Jasper took the car back and

got his sweet potato instead. And there was time for two good practices before the dancing at the new Fire Station.

At last the party was ready to begin.

Mr. Floogle lifted his arm and his comb.

Fanny Flora was bewitching with her fresh curls and her dress and just-the-right-size harmonica.

Amos' slide whistle was gleaming and sliding.

Fifth Cousin Jasper was handsome in a new red tie he had bought to show under his sweet potato.

Mrs. Floogle had the black keys and the white keys all straightened out in her mind.

Snitkin, just so he could enjoy the party without getting his ears hurt, wore Amos' purple plush ear muffs. And very jaunty he looked.

Mr. Floogle swung the orchestra into a fine Grand March, and away went the party. It was a *splendid* party. Jigs and polkas and waltzes, and no confusing which was which.

Mr. Floogle encouraged Fifth Cousin Jasper to play two solos on the sweet potato, which was only fair. After all, Fifth Cousin Jasper had helped the Floogles with a *very* confusing problem.

Besides, he had solemnly promised never, *never, NEVER* to tell about Mr. Floogle's violin or Amos' cornet or Fanny Flora's harp. Or the piano that sounded so loud because there was nothing else to sound at all.

4: The Floogles Are Detectives

Everything always happens to the Floogles! Like the time Mrs. Floogle bought the dressmaker's dummy at the rummage sale, and Mr. Floogle's Cousin Oscar came to visit just at the wrong time, and Amos Floogle found a book that told all about being a detective. All these things got all mixed up together, until no one was quite sure who was coming and who was going.

Mrs. Floogle came home from the rummage sale, her face full of smiles and her arms full of dressmaker's dummy.

"This will be wonderful," she said happily. "Now I will have something to try my dresses on while I am making them. And how I have wanted that! It is very confusing never to know how a dress will look until the last stitch is in. Especially if it turns out that the dress looks quite awful."

So Mr. Floogle and Amos and Fanny Flora were very pleased about the dressmaker's dummy. So was Snitkin, after he got used to having it around.

But then it turned out that Mrs. Floogle didn't fit the dressmaker's dummy, and the dressmaker's dummy didn't fit Mrs. Floogle. And the rummage sale simply would not take the dummy back.

So Mr. Floogle carried the dummy up to the attic until Fanny Flora should grow up to fit it. And nothing whatever was said about dressmakers or dressmakers' dummies. Mrs. Floogle put the cover over the sewing machine, and her mouth was tight at the edges.

The next day Mr. Floogle's Cousin Oscar

came for a short visit. Mrs. Floogle gave him the bedroom right over the kitchen, for it was certainly the pleasantest and the most comfortable.

"It isn't that I don't like Cousin Oscar," said Mrs. Floogle when the dishes were done and Cousin Oscar was tucked in bed. "He is a lovely, kind person."

"But?" asked Mr. Floogle, scratching his worried head.

"But Cousin Oscar is so shy!" cried Mrs. Floogle.

"Not with us," said Amos and Fanny Flora. "With us he makes kites and dams up the brook and peels an apple with one long peel."

"No, not with you," said Mrs. Floogle. "But with everyone else."

"Agreed," said Mr. Floogle. "But what of that?"

"The dance!" said Mrs. Floogle. "The wonderful, exciting, marvelous barn dance in Charley Haverstack's new barn next week! I have a new dress, and Fanny Flora has a new dress and new hair bows too. Amos has new shoes, and Snitkin has a new collar."

"And I have a fine red necktie," said Mr. Floogle proudly.

"Well, we just cannot go," said Mrs. Floogle.

"Can't go?" cried all the other Floogles, and Snitkin howled.

"No," said Mrs. Floogle. "We cannot be so impolite. Cousin Oscar is too shy to go to a dance. And we cannot go if Cousin Oscar does not go."

And all the Floogles were sad. For Charley Haverstack's new barn was full of fresh paint and clean hay and fine smells of newness. And before Charley Haverstack's new barn was full of fine cows, Charley Haverstack was giving a fine party. There would be dancing, with a fiddler to help a man know when to swing his waltzing lady. And games, with Amos sure in his heart to win at least one prize. And supper, with Fanny Flora making her very first and very best chocolate cake to take to it.

"Oh!" said all the Floogles.

But they said no more than that. And they never pouted or frowned. For they all loved Cousin Oscar. Besides, there was nothing to be done about it. Cousin Oscar was too shy—much too shy—to go to Charley Haverstack's party.

So Amos said he had to get on with his detecting and went off to read the book he'd been so fortunate to find that morning. It was a very worth-while book indeed, for it told about clues and fingerprints and bloodhounds and such.

Amos said no detective would dream of being a detective without a book like this one. Fanny Flora said she was going to be a detective, too. Amos said Snitkin could be a bloodhound. But Snitkin made up his mind he positively would *not* be a bloodhound.

And that night, when everyone was asleep, IT began.

Softly. Softly. Shh, shh, shh. And a tiny thread of whistle.

Amos decided he was cold, and put his head under the covers. Fanny Flora decided girls were practically never detectives. Snitkin made up his mind right then and there he'd *never* be a bloodhound. And Mrs. Floogle said to Mr. Floogle, "What's that?"

"Mice," said Mr. Floogle comfortably. But he didn't believe it either.

The next morning, with the sun shining in and out the ruffled curtains and everyone full of pancakes and little sausages, Mrs. Floogle decided maybe there had been mice. And Amos wondered why in the world he'd got so cold. And Fanny Flora thought perhaps she would enjoy being a detective. But Snitkin was determined not to be a bloodhound.

Amos and Fanny Flora had a wonderful

morning with Cousin Oscar, for they went to the woods to see what there was to be seen.

But that afternoon Cousin Oscar was tired as could be and had to take a nap before supper.

Supper was good, and Cousin Oscar was gay. He told many a fine story about the days when he and Mr. Floogle were boys.

Then everyone went happily to bed.

And then IT began again.

A little faster. A little louder. A little bolder. Shuff, shuff, shuff. Click, click, click. And a tiny thread of whistle.

"What's that?" asked Mrs. Floogle.

"Rats," said Mr. Floogle comfortably. But he didn't believe it either.

And Amos and Fanny Flora decided it was *cold* and pulled their chins and their noses and their eyes and their hair under the covers. Snitkin, too, decided it was cold, especially for a dog that wasn't a bloodhound. So Amos found room for Snitkin in his bed.

The next morning, with the dew making diamonds in the spider webs and everyone full of waffles and bacon, Mrs. Floogle decided maybe there had been rats. Amos decided it was much warmer. Fanny Flora decided she would read Amos' book, since she was going to be a detective, too. But Snitkin was sure he wasn't going to be a bloodhound.

Amos and Fanny Flora had a wonderful morning with Cousin Oscar, for they went to the old bridge over the river and caught five fish for lunch.

But Cousin Oscar was tired as could be that afternoon and had to take a nap before supper.

That evening was the jolliest the Floogles had ever known. They popped corn over the fire, and Cousin Oscar told many a story of lumberjack days in the North.

At last they went happily to bed.

And then IT began . . . again.

Much faster. Much louder. Much bolder. Shufflety, shufflety, shuff. Clickety, clickety, clack. And a tiny thread of whistle.

"What's that?" asked Mrs. Floogle.

"Squirrels," said Mr. Floogle comfortably. But he didn't believe it either.

And Amos and Fanny Flora and Snitkin decided they'd never been so *cold in all their lives.*

But the next morning, with the morning glories peeping through the trellis and everyone full of ham and fried eggs, Mrs. Floogle decided maybe there had been squirrels. Amos and Fanny Flora decided detectives were never cold. But Snitkin was positive he wasn't going to be a bloodhound.

Amos and Fanny Flora had a wonderful morning with Cousin Oscar, for they went to town and helped him with his shopping. Cousin Oscar had suddenly made up his mind he must own at once a beautiful blue tie and a white shirt to go with it.

Cousin Oscar was tired as could be that afternoon and had to take a nap. Mr. Floogle and Mrs. Floogle and Amos and Fanny Flora were yawning, too, so everyone had a short nap before supper.

That evening was even happier than the one before. Cousin Oscar showed the Floogles the secret of pulling taffy, and he showed Amos and

Fanny Flora the secret of making pennies come out of their ears.

So at last everyone went happily to bed.

And then IT began . . . *again.*

Very fast. Very loud. Very bold. Whoosh-whoosh-whoosh. Slick, slick, slick. Hum, two, three, hum. And a tiny thread of whistle.

"What's that?" asked Mrs. Floogle. "Elephants?"

"Well, no," said Mr. Floogle.

Mrs. Floogle didn't really think it was elephants either.

Amos decided that a brave detective *never* got cold. Fanny Flora wished she could peek in the detective book just once more. Snitkin absolutely and finally made up his mind not to be a bloodhound.

"But after all—!" growled Snitkin deep in his throat. He got up. He padded softly and he padded quietly and he padded with his teeth ready toward the attic.

Amos, with just one tiny last shiver, picked up his flashlight and put his detecting book under his arm and started toward the attic.

Fanny Flora picked up *her* flashlight and her special detective magnifying glass and started toward the attic.

Mrs. Floogle said, "Elephants, squirrels, rats and mice, indeed!" And she followed Mr. Floogle and his flashlight toward the attic. She carried with her a most wonderfully polished baseball bat she had bought for Amos' birthday surprise.

Tiptoe, tiptoe, tiptoe! went the Floogles.

Shoosh, shoosh, shoosh! went their slippered feet.

Thump, thump, thump! went their frightened hearts.

"Now!" cried each Floogle to himself.

And they flashed on the flashlights.

Mr. Floogle's light picked up Fanny Flora,

and Mrs. Floogle had to hang on hard to stop the baseball bat's swing.

Fanny Flora's light picked up Amos.

Amos' light picked up Snitkin and his shining, sharp teeth.

But the moonlight silvering the attic windows picked up—Cousin Oscar! Cousin Oscar, whistling a gay little thread of whistle. Cousin Oscar, graceful as a barn swallow, quick as a cricket, frisky as a spring lamb, happy as a lark. Cousin Oscar, bowing and turning and gliding. Cousin Oscar, waltzing with the dressmaker's dummy!

"COUSIN OSCAR!" thundered Mr. Floogle.

So Cousin Oscar made a very fine bow from the waist to the dressmaker's dummy and smiled on the Floogles with no shyness at all.

"It's Charley Haverstack's barn dance tomorrow," said Cousin Oscar. "With a fiddler to help a man know when to swing his waltzing

lady. With games, and Amos sure to win a prize. And supper, and Fanny Flora making her first chocolate cake. Charley Haverstack's wonderful party you were going to miss, all because of me and my shyness."

"How did you know?" cried Mrs. Floogle. "We said never a word to you about it."

"And never a pout or a frown, either," said Cousin Oscar. "But talk travels fast and talk travels easily, especially through the stovepipe hole from the kitchen to my comfortable room. And I heard you that night you decided you'd stay home because of my shyness."

Cousin Oscar smiled a good smile at them all. "It seemed to me that if you could give up a party for me, I could give up my shyness for you. And so I have been learning to waltz with Miss Mehitabel Jones—" he bowed gallantly to the dressmaker's dummy—"who is an elegant waltzer, although a bit stiff and clumsy in making a turn."

So Mrs. Floogle kindly offered to waltz with Cousin Oscar. They flew with grace and light feet across the moonlit floor while Mr. Floogle whistled the gayest waltz any fiddler could ever fiddle.

And then the Floogles hurried down from the attic to get on with their sleeping, for there was much to be done in the morning.

They hurried and they scurried and, after supper next evening, they were ready—Cousin Oscar in his new white shirt and blue tie, Mr. Floogle very gay in his red tie, Mrs. Floogle and Fanny Flora in their new dresses, Amos a-shine in his new shoes and Snitkin very handsome in his new collar.

Cousin Oscar, being company and Mr. Floogle's cousin, carried Fanny Flora's very first chocolate cake, which was certainly the best that could be brought to a party.

As they walked to Charley Haverstack's new barn, Amos decided he'd give the detecting book to a friend, since he'd made up his mind to be just like Cousin Oscar.

Fanny Flora decided to give up being a detective and be a chocolate-cake cook instead. Cousin Oscar said he was sure she made the best chocolate cake in the whole world.

And Snitkin, his head up high so that no one could fail to see his beautiful collar, made up his mind absolutely, positively, completely and without a doubt that he would never, *never* be a bloodhound—or anything else except Snitkin Floogle.

5: The Floogles Have Thanksgiving Dinner

The air was cold and the air was frosty. Squashes were piled up in the barn, and the pumpkins were more gold than gold could be. Thanksgivingtime was coming, bringing the good dinners and the mince pies and the little candies in paper cups.

Amos and Fanny Flora Floogle were reading at school about the Pilgrims and the first Thanksgiving and the friendly Indians.

At home Mr. Floogle and Mrs. Floogle listened carefully when Amos told them about the first Thanksgiving.

Mr. Floogle was especially pleased about Squanto.

"That trick of burying a fish with the corn was certainly a good one," said Mr. Floogle. "We might try it next year. Squanto was just as smart as he was helpful."

"Ah, the poor dears!" said Mrs. Floogle. "Not much of a feast they had, was it?"

"The best they could cook," said Amos.

"Of course, of course," said Mrs. Floogle. "What with all the sickness and trouble and being in a new country and not having their gardens growing well. All I meant was that we certainly do better."

And then the Floogles got their wonderful idea for a Thanksgiving party for the Pilgrims.

"After all, the Pilgrims never had a really bang-up Thanksgiving feast," said Mrs. Floogle.

Mr. Floogle said he just wanted to be sure nobody forgot to invite Squanto. There were a lot of things Squanto knew about growing corn. They could have a good talk.

Fanny Flora said they should be sure to invite the teacher.

Amos decided he'd better brush up on sign language, what with Indians coming and all.

Then the work began.

Mrs. Floogle and Fanny Flora cleaned the house from top to bottom. Mr. Floogle and Amos helped carry the mattresses in and the pillows out.

"The Pilgrims will be wanting to look all around the house," Mrs. Floogle explained, "after all those years of log cabins and puncheon floors and uncomfortable beds to sleep on."

So the Floogles worked with a right good will. They did not want a fluff of dust to be found in their house at the Thanksgiving party.

Then the pie making began. Pumpkin pies along the cellar stairs. Mince pies along the cellar windows. Apple pies along the porch railing. Snitkin had a hard time remembering his manners.

And the nut cracking! Walnuts on Sunday night. Pecans on Monday night. Peanuts on Tuesday night. Hazelnuts on Wednesday night. Almonds on Thursday night. Pistachios on Friday night. More peanuts on Saturday night.

And the baking! Fourteen loaves of crusty bread. Thirteen pans of crusty rolls. Four round cakes with chocolate frosting. Three square cakes with maple frosting. Twenty-two cupcakes to eat in-between times.

And the turkeys! All the turkeys that would fit in the oven. Plump in the legs and white in the wings, with skin to turn crisp and golden from the heat of the fire.

And the stuffing! Sage and bread crumbs and celery and raisins and onions, and chestnuts besides.

"Heigh-ho," said Mrs. Floogle at last. "We're ready. Such a Thanksgiving dinner there never was. Such a Thanksgiving dinner there never will be again.

"Fanny Flora and Amos must tell the teacher tomorrow."

Fanny Flora and Amos said they would.

Mr. Floogle said to be sure not to forget about Squanto. In fact, Mr. Floogle thought it would be a good idea to write everything down in a note. So they did. Fanny Flora did the copying since she wrote very prettily, and Mrs. Floogle gave a beautiful hand-painted envelope left over from last year's Fourth-of-July fireworks.

Next morning Amos and Fanny Flora set out happily for school. They were very careful not to leave thumb prints on the envelope.

Mr. Floogle and Mrs. Floogle stayed at home and waited.

At noon, almost before Amos and Fanny Flora got in the door, Mrs. Floogle took off her apron and said, "Are they coming? Are they *all* coming?"

But Amos looked sad. And Fanny Flora looked unhappy.

"Oh, oh!" said Mr. Floogle. "Trouble with Squanto?"

Amos and Fanny Flora were too unhappy and embarrassed to speak.

"Come, come," said Mrs. Floogle. "I've a dinner to cook tomorrow. How many are coming?"

"None," said Fanny Flora.

"Except the teacher," said Amos.

"Why?" asked Mrs. Floogle.

"Dead," said Fanny Flora.

"Dead?" asked Mr. Floogle.

"Except the teacher," said Amos. "The Pilgrims and the first Thanksgiving and Squanto and the fish were all back in 1620."

"Good gracious!" said Mrs. Floogle. "That's before our time. That's even before Big Grandfather's time."

"That's more than three hundred years ago," said Mr. Floogle. He was *very* quick at arithmetic, as long as there weren't any fractions.

"Oh, my!" said all the Floogles.

"I think it very odd that the teacher did not tell you," said Mrs. Floogle.

Amos hung his head. "She did, but we forgot."

"Oh, well," said Mr. Floogle. "There's no use crying over spilled milk. We had better save our tears for that enormous stomach-ache we are sure to have after that enormous Thanksgiving dinner tomorrow. I shall miss Squanto, though."

After supper, which was quite a sad meal, for the Floogles had had their hearts set on a party, the teacher came to the Floogles' kitchen.

The Floogles tried to pretend that the mistake didn't matter a bit, and that they had known about 1620 all along, and that it was an excellent joke, and that they didn't care in the slightest.

But the teacher saw all the pies and all the cakes and all the rolls and all the loaves of bread and all the nuts and all the turkeys and all the stuffing and all the sad Floogles pretending so hard. She rubbed her cheek and her chin and then she said, "There are others besides the Pilgrims who have bad years and poor homes and gardens that did not grow well."

"Why, of course!" shouted Mr. Floogle.

"Certainly," agreed Mrs. Floogle.

And the Floogles smiled happily with no pretending at all.

Amos hopped on his bicycle and Fanny Flora rode with him, and they raced here and they raced there, and they took notes to this house and they took notes to that house.

When they got home, Mr. Floogle and Mrs. Floogle and the teacher were waiting, and the twenty-two cupcakes were nearly gone.

"Everyone," promised Amos and Fanny Flora. "Everyone's coming tomorrow!"

So the Floogles' Thanksgiving dinner was a happy one, with the enormous stomach-ache fairly divided. For, though the Pilgrims could not come, instead came all the people for miles around who'd had a hard year or a sick year or a just-getting-started year.

Mrs. Floogle carried in the great turkeys, and she was happy.

Amos cut the pies, and he was happy.

Fanny Flora made the cranberry sauce, and she was happy.

Mr. Floogle did miss Squanto, for he had set great store on getting his advice about corn. But as it turned out, the man four chairs away did a great deal of fishing in his spare time. He very kindly offered to bring a string of fish now and then to bury in Mr. Floogle's cornfield. So Mr. Floogle was happy, and he carved the white meat and he carved the dark with a right good will and a sharp, sharp knife.

6: The Floogles
Paint the Flagpole

One fine spring day Mr. Floogle came home from the town. His eyes were flashing, and his hair was bristling and his pipe was puffing enormous clouds of blue smoke. Mr. Floogle was angry. Mr. Floogle was *tremendously* angry.

"You know the flagpole in front of the Courthouse?" said Mr. Floogle.

Of course Mrs. Floogle and Fanny Flora and Amos knew the flagpole in front of the Courthouse, although they said they hadn't given it any special attention lately.

"Well, *I* have!" said Mr. Floogle. "Today,

when I took Snitkin to the Courthouse for his license to be a dog.

"Such a flagpole! The gold ball on the top is so rained-on and snowed-on with no polishing between times that it cannot sparkle in the brightest sun. And the flagpole is dark with weather and chimney smoke of winter and bonfires of autumn.

"Such a place for our flag!" And Mr. Floogle got quite red in the face, just thinking about it.

"The problem is very simple," said Mrs. Floogle. "After a good supper, you must stroll along to the Mayor's house and tell him about the flagpole."

Mr. Floogle smiled fondly at Mrs. Floogle and said she was a remarkable woman with an enormous amount of good sense. Then he sat down to enjoy his fine, hot supper. When the dishes were finished, Mr. Floogle strolled through the blue dusk to the Mayor's house.

But he came home much sooner than he had expected.

"The Mayor says there is no money for flag-pole painting!" shouted Mr. Floogle.

"The Mayor says there is no money for gold-ball polishing," shouted Mr. Floogle.

"The Mayor says—!"

"But what did you say?" asked Mrs. Floogle. "That is the most important thing."

"I said *we* would polish the gold ball and paint the flagpole," said Mr. Floogle.

"Of course," said Amos.

"Quite right," said Mrs. Floogle.

"How?" asked Fanny Flora.

"Very simple," said Mr. Floogle. "The Floo-gles have always been good climbers. Ever since my Great-grandfather Floogle became a mountain climber."

Amos pointed out that the night was silvered with the moon and the shadows were small. So the Floogles decided happily to paint the flag-pole in the secret hours for a surprise.

"Tomorrow morning there will be the fine flagpole," said Mr. Floogle.

Mrs. Floogle bustled off to mix up a batch of her Cousin Ermintrude's special polish for pol-ishing gold balls.

Mr. Floogle collected the paint and the brushes and the turpentine.

It was decided that Mr. Floogle would climb up to the top and do the gold-ball polishing. Amos would paint the flagpole from the top to the middle and Fanny Flora would paint from the middle to the bottom.

Mrs. Floogle was to stay on the ground and have complete charge of mixing the paint, count-ing the paint rags and pouring the turpentine.

Snitkin's job was to chase off any cats that might suddenly think it pleasant to climb the flagpole.

This sensible plan was agreed upon, and Mr.

Floogle and Amos and Fanny Flora began their climb up the pole.

"Coming down will be *much* easier," puffed Mr. Floogle encouragingly as he pulled and hauled and wrestled himself up to the gold ball.

"I should hope so," muttered Fanny Flora. She was a little cross, which was natural enough. Amos kept banging his pail of paint while he was climbing, and the drops were forever splashing on Fanny Flora's nose.

At last the Floogles were ready: Mr. Floogle at the top with the gold-ball polish, Amos just below with white paint and a brush, Fanny Flora at the middle with her white paint and brush.

"Let's get to work," called Mr. Floogle happily. "Soon we'll have a beautiful white flagpole for our flag."

Fanny Flora painted a little, and slid down the pole a little to paint some more. Amos painted a little, and slid down the pole a little to paint some

more. Mr. Floogle stayed where he was to polish. Mrs. Floogle stood safe on the ground and
admired.

Finally the Floogles had finished.

Fanny Flora had painted all of her half from
the middle to the bottom. So she was on the
ground. Amos had painted his half from the top
to the middle. So he was at the middle. Mr.
Floogle had polished the gold ball. So he was at
the top.

"All through!" cried Amos happily. He relaxed his grip on the pole and slid to the ground
like a fireman.

"All through!" cried Mr. Floogle happily.
And he relaxed his grip on the gold ball and
slid to the ground like a fireman.

"Oh, oh, oh!" cried Mrs. Floogle and Fanny
Flora—and Amos and Mr. Floogle, too, when
they saw what had happened. For Fanny Flora's
paint was off the flagpole and on Amos' legs.

And Amos' paint was off the flagpole and on Mr. Floogle's legs.

"Goodness gracious, my oh me!" cried Mrs. Floogle.

All the Floogles were quite upset. Fanny Flora tried to be cheerful and pointed to the polished gold ball shining in the moonlight. But Amos and Mr. Floogle said the paint made their legs itch.

Mrs. Floogle said, *"Something* must be done! The flagpole looks worse than ever. The shining gold ball at the top makes the rest look worse than it did before."

The other Floogles agreed that something had to be done.

"The thing to do," said Mr. Floogle, "is to arrange our painting so that no one has to slide over wet paint."

The Floogles agreed to this sensible rule.

"So," said Mr. Floogle, "we need a saw."

Amos obligingly ran home and got Mr.

Floogle's best saw. Then Mr. Floogle carefully sawed off the flagpole, with the rest of the Floogles pushing and pulling so that the pole would not fall on the Courthouse and knock over the chimney.

"The Mayor would be quite annoyed," Mr. Floogle explained.

As it happened, by careful planning and plenty of pushing and pulling, the Floogles got the flagpole down with no accidents at all. Except one window that got broken because no one had noticed it. This, it turned out later, was a window nobody had been able to open for seventeen years, and the Mayor was very relieved to have some fresh air.

"Now!" said Mr. Floogle when the flagpole was stretched out on the ground. "Now we can paint without anyone doing any sliding."

So the Floogles picked up their paint brushes and painted happily and thought how clever Mr. Floogle was.

When one side was finished the Floogles rolled the flagpole over and painted the other side, being careful, of course, not to drip on the polished gold ball.

"After all," the Floogles told one another, "we must keep things neat."

When the painting was finished the Floogles were *very* happy and pleased.

"Now we'll lift it into its proper place again," said Mr. Floogle. So they lifted, first putting on gloves to keep fingerprints off the shining gold ball.

But when they lifted—oh my! The Sheriff, who had lent his handcuffs to a friend for the afternoon, had spent his time mowing the grass. But, since he had had to go hunting for the handcuff key, he had not had time to rake up the pieces of grass he had cut. Now they were stuck, every one, to the fresh paint on the flagpole.

"Goodness gracious me!" cried Mrs. Floogle. "One side of our flagpole has grown hair!"

"Green hair!" cried Fanny Flora.

"Grass," explained Mr. Floogle wisely.

"Oh, my! What shall we do now?" said the Floogles sadly. They were so near to tears that they could taste the salt.

Then Fanny Flora spoke up bravely. "We must saw," she said. And she showed the Floogles how.

One piece stood up nicely and was as tall as Mrs. Floogle could reach.

One piece stood steady, as tall as Mr. Floogle could reach.

One piece for Fanny Flora and one piece for Amos.

"And *don't knock ANYTHING over*," said Mr. Floogle.

So the Floogles painted busily and the Floogles painted hopefully. When they were done, the moon was tired and the first morning breeze stirred a ripple in the leaves. The quietness before night becomes day was like a soft blanket.

The Floogles put down their paint brushes.

"Now," whispered the Floogles, "now we will put the pieces together."

Suddenly Snitkin, who had waited patiently through the moonlit night without any supper, made up his mind.

Snitkin dearly loved Mr. Floogle and Mrs. Floogle and Amos and Fanny Flora. But even Snitkin had to admit that the Floogles moved fast, too fast, around wet paint. Especially Mr. Floogle.

So Snitkin made up his mind. After all, soon it would be morning. Anyone knows that the flag must float in the first few sunbeams of the morning. There was no more time for wiping paint off and painting paint on. Besides, Snitkin had no wish at all to miss his breakfast along with his supper.

So Snitkin did what he never before had done

to a Floogle—he *growled!* Hard. Deep in his throat. Unfriendly.

Snitkin walked up and down, up and down, in front of the pieces of flagpole. Snitkin was a lion. Snitkin was a tiger. The Floogles dared not touch the flagpole. The Floogles stared at Snitkin.

"Snitkin? Growling? *Our* Snitkin!" cried the Floogles, and they could not believe what they saw.

Snitkin's heart ached. But he growled. Snitkin was a lion, a tiger. The Floogles stayed back.

The minutes ticked by. Birds called softly to the day, and darkness melted from the sky and slid gently from the buildings. Then Snitkin jumped and barked and wiggled his tail and sat up nicely and gave Amos his paw.

"Well, of course!" cried Mr. Floogle. "Snitkin made us wait till the paint was dry!"

Then the Floogles hurried and hurried. A

screw here, a bolt there, and a good big nail in the middle.

"Up she goes!" cried Mr. Floogle at last.

Up went the flagpole. Not a paint smear. Not a finger mark. Not a stuck-on blade of grass. Shining white from top to bottom and purest gold on the top for the sun's first rays.

Then the Floogles patted Snitkin, and Amos bought a hamburger with his allowance and fed every bite to Snitkin.

"We've done a hard night's work." Mrs. Floogle yawned.

"But Snitkin had the hardest job of all," said Mr. Floogle. "To do a good job is hard work. But to do a good job when people do not understand you are trying to help—that is the hardest work of all."

All the Floogles petted Snitkin again and said that Mr. Floogle was absolutely right.

When the Mayor saw the wonderful flagpole surprise he called up the Sheriff and the Fire

Department and the Boy Scouts. And the bugler blew while the flag rose to the top of the gleaming pole. People cheered and clapped, and the Fire Department band played a good march.

Then the Mayor drove the Floogles home in the fire truck, and asked in a puzzled voice, "Where in the world did you get such extraordinarily white, white legs?"

Amos did not say. Mr. Floogle did not say. Neither did Mrs. Floogle or Fanny Flora. For the Floogles decided right then and there they never, *never, NEVER* would tell they'd used seventeen quarts of good white paint—four quarts on the flagpole and the rest on the Floogles.

"We might have needed a dozen quarts more if Snitkin had not made up his mind," said the Floogles to one another. And they gave him a very fine breakfast before they started scrubbing off the white paint.

A few days later Mr. Floogle's uncle's nephew

came visiting on Mr. Floogle's birthday. Being a sailor himself on a fishing schooner, he was well acquainted with masts and spars and was able to tell the Floogles how the flagpole *should* have been painted. But nobody cared whether the Floogles had painted the right way or the wrong way. For, as the sailor himself said, all the town could be proud of the fine flagpole and the flag that waved and rippled over the Court-house.

7: The Floogles Are Shipwrecked

Mr. Floogle *loves* fish. Fish in the aquarium. Fish on his fish line. Fish in the frying pan. Makes no difference to Mr. Floogle.

"I never get enough of them to eat," says Mr. Floogle, very sure in his voice. "Never! I could eat fish for breakfast, fish for lunch, fish for supper and fish again before I go to bed."

So one day Mrs. Floogle's Fifth Cousin Jasper came for supper, and he said, "Such a man for fish should go fishing."

Mr. Floogle said that was certainly true. And Mrs. Floogle and Amos and Fanny Flora said that was certainly true, too.

And Mrs. Floogle's Fifth Cousin Jasper said

he owned a cottage on a lake and a boat and a motor to fit it. And he gave Mr. Floogle the keys to everything.

Fifth Cousin Jasper said a good many other things, too. But Mr. Floogle was too excited to listen hard. So Fifth Cousin Jasper obligingly went home much earlier than he had planned so that the Floogles could get a good night's sleep.

Next morning the sun still yawned behind the hills, but the Floogles were packed up tight and ready to go fishing.

There were the rubber boots, in case they might come in handy.

There were the four fish poles, one for each Floogle. Except Snitkin, of course.

There was the big picnic basket, filled to the brim with bread and butter to eat with the fish, and salt and pepper and yellow corn meal for rolling the fish in, and the largest frying pan for cooking the fish. None of the cold roast pork.

None of the cold roast beef. No, sir. The Floogles would eat the fish they caught.

There were the keys, carefully counted, carefully strung on Mr. Floogle's best gold watch chain. The key to the lock on the cottage. The key to the chain on the motor. The key to the padlock on the boat. Mr. Floogle counted again, just to be sure.

"All there," he said happily. "Ah, 'tis a wonderful thing to own a cottage and a boat and a motor and a lake to fish in. Especially a lake with an island."

"An island!" cried Fanny Flora. "Does Fifth Cousin Jasper own an *island?*"

"Well, not exactly," said Mr. Floogle, being honest as he should be. "But the way it works out, it's practically the same. Fifth Cousin Jasper owns a cottage. The cottage has a beach. The beach has a lake. The lake has an island."

The Floogles agreed that was almost as good as owning an island.

When they reached Fifth Cousin Jasper's cottage, it was just as Mr. Floogle had said: a cottage, a beach, a lake, an island. No Fifth Cousin Jasper, of course, for he was working on the railroad. But that made no difference at all, for Mr. Floogle had the keys.

"Here's the boat," said Amos. Mr. Floogle unlocked the padlock on the boat.

"Here's the motor!" said Fanny Flora. And Mr. Floogle unlocked the chain on the motor.

"Here's the cottage," said Mrs. Floogle. But Mr. Floogle did not unlock the door of the cottage. Who can fish in a cottage?

Fanny Flora was sure Fifth Cousin Jasper had said there were important things in the cottage. Mrs. Floogle was sure, too.

"The icebox, perhaps," said Mr. Floogle. "Nothing to do with fishing."

"The stove perhaps," said Amos. "Nothing to do with fishing."

And since Fanny Flora and Mrs. Floogle

could not remember, the Floogles arranged themselves neatly in the boat. Snitkin in the little seat in the bow where he could watch the shadowed water and dream of whales. Mrs. Floogle and Fanny Flora safely in the middle. Mr. Floogle at the back to run the motor. And Amos on the beach until he gave a great push to send the boat well out into the lake and a jump into the boat. Mr. Floogle pulled one-two-three on the motor.

Chug-a-chug-a-chug and *putt-putt-puttputt-puttputt* went the motor.

"Avast!" cried Mr. Floogle, like a true sailor. And away they went, skimming over the lake to catch fish and fish and more fish.

"Haven't we enough?" asked Mrs. Floogle at last.

But Mr. Floogle said he was *very* fond of fish.

"Enough?" asked Fanny Flora an hour later.

But Mr. Floogle pointed out that he was extraordinarily fond of fish.

"Enough?" asked Amos two hours later.

This time, before Mr. Floogle could shake his head, Mrs. Floogle spoke up. "Enough!" she said. "I am hungry."

"Ah, well," said Mr. Floogle, agreeable as could be. "We can fish again after lunch." So he started the motor.

Chug-a-chug-a-chug and *putt-putt-puttputt-putt* sang the motor. And the Floogles went skimming over the silvered lake toward Fifth Cousin Jasper's cottage.

"This is the life," said Mr. Floogle. All the Floogles agreed with him. But suddenly the motor went *putt-putt—putt——chug——chug ...chug.* Very slowly. Very heavily. Very tiredly.

"Oh, my!" said Mrs. Floogle.

"Something wrong," said Mr. Floogle wisely.

"The motor!" said Amos and Fanny Flora.

The island was quite near. So Mr. Floogle steered the tired boat to its sandy beach.

Fanny Flora and Mrs. Floogle climbed out and sat on the sandy beach. Amos and Mr. Floogle looked at the motor.

They looked carefully at the bottom.

They looked carefully at the top.

They looked carefully at every side.

Fanny Flora said, "Look in the gas tank."

There was no gasoline in it.

Then Mrs. Floogle remembered. "*That* was the important thing my Fifth Cousin Jasper said was in the cottage—a bright-red can of gasoline for the motor."

"Oh, well!" said Mr. Floogle. "A little exercise is good for anyone. We will row our boat. Amos can row with one oar. I can row with the other oar."

All the Floogles cheered up immensely while Amos looked for the oars.

"No oars," said Amos at last.

Then Fanny Flora remembered. "That was the other important thing Fifth Cousin Jasper said to find in the cottage—oars for the boat."

"We are shipwrecked!" said Mr. Floogle.

"On a desert island!" shouted Amos.

"What shall we do?" cried Fanny Flora.

"Have lunch," decided Mrs. Floogle bravely.

So Mr. Floogle took the scales off the fish. Fanny Flora spread out the lunch cloth. Mrs. Floogle got the big frying pan out of the picnic basket, and the corn meal and the salt and pepper, and the bread and butter. Amos and Snitkin raced up and down the beach, as shipwrecked sailors always do, to find firewood.

After lunch, Mr. Floogle lighted his pipe and said happily, "I do like fish. Why, I could eat fish three times a day."

"You may very well be eating it three times a day," said Mrs. Floogle, "if we don't find some way of getting off this island."

But Mr. Floogle would not worry.

The island was pleasant.

The sun was warm.

The sand was comfortable.

"Being shipwrecked is not so bad," said Mr. Floogle. And he decided to take a short nap before he worried his brain about leaving the island.

When he woke up, the sun was a fiery ball, low in the sky. The Floogles did not like being shipwrecked any more.

"I am very tall," said Mr. Floogle after a good deal of careful thought. "Perhaps the water is not so deep as I am tall. I will walk to Fifth Cousin Jasper's cottage and get the can of gasoline."

So Mr. Floogle put on the rubber boots and kissed everyone good-by and made everyone promise to wait for him, which was an easy promise to make. Then he stepped into the water.

Mr. Floogle walked. The water lapped his ankles. "Not deep at all," said Mr. Floogle.

Mr. Floogle walked on. The water rippled at his knees. "Very fine," said Mr. Floogle.

Mr. Floogle walked farther. Little waves danced around his gold watch chain. "Not too bad," called Mr. Floogle.

Mr. Floogle walked on. Now the water slipped over his chest.

Mr. Floogle took a few more steps. The water

tickled him under his chin. "Not another step!" cried Mr. Floogle.

Mrs. Floogle was greatly relieved to have Mr. Floogle come back to the island. Mr. Floogle was greatly relieved to find his old bathing suit in the bottom of the picnic basket. He put it on and spread his wet clothes on a handy bush to dry.

But Fanny Flora said she would not be greatly relieved until she was safely off the island. In the secret corners of their hearts, Mr. Floogle and Mrs. Floogle and Amos and Snitkin agreed. They were all quite gloomy.

"Snitkin is a fine swimmer," Amos suggested at last. "Snitkin can carry things in his teeth. He can swim to Fifth Cousin Jasper's cottage. He can bring the can of gasoline in his teeth. I will go with him to show him the way."

Mr. Floogle said *he* would offer to go with Snitkin. But since he could not swim, he thought it would be a silly offer to make.

Since his clothes were nearly dry, Mr. Floogle put them on and lent Amos his bathing suit, which was considerably larger than Amos.

After tying a string here and a string there on the bathing suit, Amos stepped into the water with Snitkin. Snitkin paddled bravely. When the water was deep enough, Amos paddled bravely, too.

It was good that Snitkin could carry things in his teeth. For the next thing the Floogles knew, Snitkin was paddling to shore with Mr. Floogle's bathing suit in his teeth and Amos inside the bathing suit.

"I forgot that I can swim fifty yards and not a yard farther," said Amos when he'd got his breath.

Mr. Floogle and Mrs. Floogle were greatly relieved to have Amos back on the island again, and they made a great fuss over Snitkin. Snitkin enjoyed being petted, but in his heart he decided he would prefer a large slice of roast beef.

The rest of the Floogles would have liked cold roast beef, too, but they built another fire and cooked some more fish.

Mr. Floogle did not say he loved fish.

Mr. Floogle did not say he could eat fish three times a day.

Mr. Floogle did not say he wanted fish for breakfast.

Instead, he said, "Perhaps we could paddle the boat with our hands."

"Of course!" said all the other Floogles.

So they got into the boat, and they put their hands in the water and they tried to paddle.

The boat did not go far. Mostly it went in circles.

The sky grew dark and the water grew dark, for the moon was slim.

"At least we knew where we were when we were on the island," said Mrs. Floogle.

So Amos and Mr. Floogle jumped into the

water and pulled the boat back to the island. And, oh, the Floogles were a sad, sad family!

Snitkin looked at the slim moon and howled.

Fanny Flora looked at the dark water and sobbed.

Mrs. Floogle felt tight in her throat.

Amos tried hard not to think of the bright lights at home and the cold roast beef in the icebox.

"Come, come!" cried Mr. Floogle, very loud, very firm past the lump in his throat. "Floogles may be wrong. Floogles may be confused. But Floogles are always brave."

That was certainly true. So they built up a fine, big fire to hold back the dark and the cold. They decided to tell stories to pass the time away.

"No ghost stories, though," said Fanny Flora, and the rest of the Floogles agreed.

Mr. Floogle had got just past the middle of his story when someone said, "Having a picnic?"

"No, we're shipwrecked," explained Mr. Floogle. He went on with his story.

Right in the most exciting part Mr. Floogle opened his mouth and closed it again.

"Who said that?" cried Mr. Floogle.

"I did!" And into the firelight stepped Mrs. Floogle's Fifth Cousin Jasper.

"What are you doing here?" asked Mrs. Floogle. "Don't you know we're shipwrecked?"

"We forgot the oars," said Amos.

"We forgot the can of gasoline," said Fanny Flora.

"The water was too deep for me to wade in," said Mr. Floogle.

"And too wide for me to swim across," said Amos.

"Our arms were too short to paddle," said Mrs. Floogle.

"So we are shipwrecked on this island," said Fanny Flora. "And what are you doing here?"

"I came to the cottage for a fish supper," said

Fifth Cousin Jasper. "You were not there. The boat was not there. But the oars were, and the gasoline was. Then I saw your fire. So I walked across the bridge."

"The *bridge?*" shouted the Floogles.

And Mrs. Floogle's Fifth Cousin Jasper took the Floogles to the other side of the island and pointed to the fine, strong bridge.

The Floogles looked at one another.

The Floogles got red in the face.

The Floogles could not help giggling—and laughing and doubling up with laughter.

And Fifth Cousin Jasper promised he would never, *never, NEVER* tell about the time the Floogles got so confused that they were ship-wrecked on an island with a splendid bridge.

Fortunately Fifth Cousin Jasper had brought the can of gasoline with him. In no time at all the Floogles and the boat and the fish poles and the rubber boots and the picnic basket were safely home again.

Mrs. Floogle sliced the cold roast of beef, and everybody made sandwiches and drank hot cocoa.

Mr. Floogle got out the big book he had for important information and wrote, "When you are shipwrecked on a desert island, do not wade, do not swim, do not paddle with your hands. Look for the bridge instead. This is much easier."

When he read aloud what he had written, Mrs. Floogle and Amos and Fanny Flora all agreed that Mr. Floogle certainly was clever and certainly knew just how to write down important information.

Then they all went to bed to rest up from being shipwrecked. But first Mr. Floogle gave Mrs. Floogle's Fifth Cousin Jasper the fish that were left. Mr. Floogle has never, *never*, *NEVER* again said he could eat fish every day, three times a day. Not even once a day.

8: The Floogles Get Lost

Saturday morning Snitkin Floogle got up on the wrong side of his dog bed. He hung his tail low and wore his ears long. He could not cheer himself up.

Finally he made up his mind to take a small trip.

"Life is always exciting when traveling," Snitkin thought. And he trotted off through the woods.

Breakfast time came, and the Floogles—Mr. Floogle and Mrs. Floogle, Amos and Fanny Flora—came downstairs. But not Snitkin.

"Where is Snitkin?" asked Mrs. Floogle.

"In the front yard?" asked Amos.

"In the back yard?" asked Fanny Flora.

"Under the porch and not hearing the breakfast call?" asked Mr. Floogle.

But Snitkin was not there or there or there. And Snitkin was not in the cellar or in the attic or waiting for the mailman or dozing in the clear morning sunlight.

"Snitkin's gone!" said Fanny Flora. And she could not eat her pancakes and sirup.

So Fanny Flora quietly made up her mind to go looking for Snitkin. When no one was paying attention—all chattering like magpies about Snitkin, they were—she set out. But first, of course, she thoughtfully wrapped up a fresh bone with a slice of chocolate cake, in case Snitkin should be as hungry as she was.

All this time Snitkin was traveling through the woods.

Before too many minutes had ticked by, Mrs. Floogle asked, "Where is Fanny Flora?"

So Mr. Floogle and Mrs. Floogle and Amos

looked in the front yard, looked in the back yard, looked under the porch.

Amos said to himself, Fanny Flora is gone, too. She has gone to look for Snitkin. I will go looking for Fanny Flora *and* Snitkin.

When no one was paying too much attention—Mrs. Floogle by that time was looking under the quilts for Fanny Flora—Amos set out through the woods. First, of course, he thoughtfully chose a quart of fresh milk to take, in case Snitkin and Fanny Flora should be as thirsty as he was.

All this time Snitkin was traveling through the woods, and Fanny Flora was somewhere behind.

After Mr. Floogle and Mrs. Floogle had shaken out all the quilts and looked under all the pillows for Fanny Flora, Mrs. Floogle noticed that Amos was gone.

"Oh, my!" said Mrs. Floogle, and her eyes were big and her mouth was a-tremble.

"Nothing to worry about," said Mr. Floogle bravely. "We know where everyone is. Amos has gone looking for Fanny Flora. And Fanny Flora has gone looking for Snitkin."

"True," said Mrs. Floogle, feeling more cheerful at once. "Now, if only we knew where Snitkin is!"

Mr. Floogle quietly made up his mind to go looking for Amos and Fanny Flora and Snitkin. So the minute Mrs. Floogle glanced one way, Mr. Floogle tiptoed the other. First, of course, he thoughtfully put together a dozen ham sandwiches. Just in case.

All this while Snitkin was strolling through the woods. Fanny Flora was somewhere behind, and Amos somewhere behind her.

Then the minutes pulled themselves by Mrs. Floogle.

And the hours dragged themselves by Mrs. Floogle.

And Mrs. Floogle could not, would not stand it.

So she put on her hat and buttoned her coat, and she hurried down to the station to see her Fifth Cousin Jasper.

He stopped looking at brakes on trains and listened carefully to her unhappy story.

"First Snitkin. Next Fanny Flora. Then Amos. Now Mr. Floogle," said Fifth Cousin Jasper. "This is a matter for the Mayor."

So he bustled Mrs. Floogle off to the Mayor's office, and Mrs. Floogle told the Mayor.

"A matter for the Fire Department," the Mayor decided.

So he called the Fire Chief, and the Fire Chief called the hook-and-ladder men, and they went into the woods to look for Mr. Floogle and Amos and Fanny Flora and Snitkin. The Fire Chief sent along a gallon of polish. After all, it was too much to expect the hook and ladder to travel through the woods without a scratch.

Then Mrs. Floogle and her Fifth Cousin Jasper and the Mayor and the Fire Chief waited and waited and *waited*.

By this time Snitkin had grown tired in the woods and did not know quite where to turn. Fanny Flora was tired and did not know quite where to turn. Amos was tired and did not know. Mr. Floogle, too.

"Well," said the Fire Chief at last, "Mr. Floogle has not come back. Fanny Flora has not come back. Amos hasn't. Nor Snitkin. *Nor* the hook and ladder. This is a matter for the Sheriff."

So Mrs. Floogle and her Fifth Cousin Jasper and the Mayor and the Fire Chief went to see the Sheriff.

The Sheriff was very important.

He said naturally Mrs. Floogle would not know how to go about finding her family.

He said fire engines were absolutely no good at all whatsoever for hunting in the woods.

He said he would have everyone found in a hurry.

"Sirens," he explained. "Sirens will do anything."

So the Sheriff called his two splendid police cars with sirens on the fenders. They hurried to the woods.

"OooooOOOOOooooo!" screamed one siren.

"OooooOOOOOooooo!" answered the other siren.

"Ah!" said the Sheriff happily.

"Oh!" said all the Floogles in the woods unhappily. Especially Snitkin.

Then Mrs. Floogle and her Fifth Cousin Jasper and the Mayor and the Fire Chief and the Sheriff waited and *waited* and *WAITED*.

And all this while Snitkin was very interested in getting home to the Floogles. He took to going in circles. Fanny Flora, too, and Amos and Mr. Floogle. And the hook and ladder—

though it was very hard to do. And the sirens wore out completely.

At last the Sheriff said, "This is a matter for the Governor."

So the Mayor telephoned the Governor. The Mayor said if something wasn't done soon, he would end up with the whole town in the woods, which was a silly place for the town to be.

The Governor said it certainly was. And very inconvenient, too. So the Governor thought awhile, and then he said, "The thing is to make

everybody stand still. People in the woods go
around in circles."

"Why?" asked the Mayor, who was always
interested in reasons.

"I don't know why," said the Governor quite
crossly. "They just do. Tell them to stand still."

Mrs. Floogle pointed out that they would have
to find the people to tell them to stand still. And
if they could find them to tell them, there would
be no need to tell them.

So the Governor put down the telephone and

got into his special silvery airplane and flew to the woods. First, though, he borrowed a cheer leader's megaphone.

Back and forth above the woods flew the Governor. And he leaned to the left and leaned to the right and shouted, "Floogles in the woods, stand still! Hook and ladder in the woods, stand still! Police cars with sirens, stand still!"

So Snitkin and Fanny Flora and Amos and Mr. Floogle and the hook and ladder and the police cars stood still. They did not move an inch to the right or the left. Not half an inch. Who ever disobeys the Governor?

"There!" said the Governor after he'd landed his silvery airplane. "Now you'll see. Everything will be all right. The thing to do when you're confused in the woods is to stand still."

Well, of course, Mrs. Floogle was pleased and delighted with all this help from the Governor. But she was puzzled. And, as the minutes and the half-hours and the hours went by, Mrs. Floogle grew more puzzled and more puzzled.

"If *everybody* stands still in the woods," said Mrs. Floogle at last, "and *nobody* moves, how will *anybody* get out of the woods?"

The Governor looked at the Mayor.

And the Mayor looked at the Sheriff.

The Sheriff looked at the Fire Chief.

The Fire Chief looked at Fifth Cousin Jasper.

No one knew the answer.

They all tried to think of someone to ask. But Mrs. Floogle said it was high time to stop all this nonsense. Snitkin and Fanny Flora and Amos and Mr. Floogle and the hook-and-ladder men and the police cars were certainly getting tired of standing still. Besides, she wanted to get a roast of pork out of the oven and into the Floogles.

So she went to see the piper, who was closely related to the Pied Piper of Hamelin. This piper played the flute and the penny whistle in the town's marching band. He kept three white mice in a cage, as a pretty mark of respect to his famous relation, who had been a seventeenth uncle by marriage. And he agreed to lend them and his penny whistle and himself to Mrs. Floogle.

The baker agreed to lend his tortoise-shell cat, although he said Snitkin would not enjoy the loan, being particularly unfriendly to that particular cat. But Mrs. Floogle said that was an important part of the plan. So the baker carried the cat in his arms. Mrs. Floogle carried the mice in a shoe box, for she did not like mice very well. Not even white ones.

The piper stood at one end of the woods and Mrs. Floogle and the baker at the other. And when the piper played his penny whistle, Mrs. Floogle let the three white mice out of the box.

As might be expected, they were gone in a flash.

As might be expected, they hurried and scampered and raced toward the piper's whistling—

for the piper certainly piped as well as his famous relation. (Some people said he piped better.)

The baker's tortoise-shell cat leaped from his arms to chase the mice.

She flashed through the woods past Snitkin. And Snitkin said to himself, Of all the cats I particularly do not like, the baker's tortoise-shell cat is the particular one. So Snitkin raced after the cat.

The mice and the cat and Snitkin flashed by Fanny Flora. Fanny Flora said, "Snitkin must not chase cats." So Fanny Flora raced after Snitkin.

The mice and the cat and Snitkin and Fanny Flora flashed by Amos. Amos said, "I cannot let Fanny Flora run any faster than I do." Who wants a girl to beat him? Especially his sister. So Amos raced after Fanny Flora.

The mice and the cat and Snitkin and Fanny Flora and Amos flashed by Mr. Floogle. He said, "If Amos is in such a hurry, it must be suppertime." So Mr. Floogle raced after Amos.

The mice and the cat and Snitkin and Fanny Flora and Amos and Mr. Floogle raced by the hook-and-ladder men. The hook-and-ladder men said, "If they are running to a fire, we must hurry too." So they raced in their hook and ladder after Mr. Floogle.

The mice and the cat and Snitkin and Fanny Flora and Amos and Mr. Floogle and the hook and ladder all raced past the policemen. The policemen said, "If there's a fire, the police must be there. And if there isn't a fire, the hook and ladder is speeding." So they raced after the hook and ladder.

And out of the woods they came—the mice and the cat, Snitkin and Fanny Flora, Amos and Mr. Floogle, the hook and ladder and the police cars, all in time to the piper's fancy piping on his shiny penny whistle.

The white mice rested in the piper's hat, safe

from the cat. The cat rested in the arms of the baker, safe from Snitkin. The piper looked around at the Floogles and the hook and ladder and the police cars and said with great pride that even his famous relation had never piped out a more unusual race.

And the Governor and the Mayor and the Sheriff and the Fire Chief and Fifth Cousin Jasper said that was certainly true.

Fanny Flora and Amos and Mr. Floogle were sorry to say there weren't enough ham sandwiches and milk and chocolate cake to go around. (Snitkin said nothing at all about his bone.) But Mrs. Floogle remembered her manners and said there was plenty of roast pork in the oven.

So everyone went home with the Floogles for dinner—small bits of cheese for the piper's mice, a saucer of milk for the baker's cat, a fresh bone for Snitkin, and a good roast of pork for the Governor and the Mayor and the Fire Chief and the

Sheriff and policemen and the hook-and-ladder men and Fifth Cousin Jasper and all the Floogles.

"But the first thing to do," said Mrs. Floogle, not even letting Mr. Floogle sharpen the carving knife, "is to push the wrong side of Snitkin's bed tight to the wall. Then he'll not be getting up on the wrong side again. Because he *can't*."

That seemed such a sensible idea that the Floogles pushed all the wrong sides of *all* the beds tight to the walls. From that day on the Floogles have just *had* to get out on the right side of the bed. For there is no room whatever for getting out on the wrong side.

9: Fanny Flora Gets a Kitten

Fanny Flora Floogle wanted a kitten. Oh, she wanted a kitten! Some people love bread and jam. Some people love pink lolly-pops. Some people love jelly beans. And that was the way Fanny Flora loved kittens. Gray kittens with stripes, black kittens with vests, yellow kittens with spots. Made no difference. Fanny Flora loved them all.

And the Floogles had no kitten.

"Something must be done," said Mrs. Floogle.

"Little Grandmother always has kittens," said Mr. Floogle. "Sometimes extra kittens."

"We could write a letter," said Amos.

So they did. Fanny Flora wrote, and Amos

spelled, and Mrs. Floogle remembered the address, and Mr. Floogle pasted on the stamp.

Then they waited, days and nights, nights and days. At last Little Grandmother's answer came.

She said there was a lovely kitten, just right for Fanny Flora and Amos and Mr. Floogle and Mrs. Floogle.

She said even Snitkin would like this kitten.

She said the lovely kitten would come to the Floogles on the train.

She said Big Grandfather had built a fine crate for the kitten to ride in on his trip.

She said the kitten would come the very next day.

"Splendid! Splendid!" said Mr. Floogle. "I have to meet the train anyway, and wearing my leather gloves." He looked extremely important and full of bravery. "Probably a whip, too."

"My goodness!" cried Mrs. Floogle. "Why?"

"Tiger," said Mr. Floogle, his chest high with bravery. "A little tiger is coming. For the Zoo.

The Zoo Man has a cold in his head, so I offered to met the train *and* the tiger. The tiger will be in a crate, of course. Still ... "

And Mr. Floogle went out to the barn to look around for the horsewhip he'd bought at the county fair years ago. Mrs. Floogle had always said it was a silly thing to buy, for they had no horse. And what Floogle would whip a horse even if he had one? But now with a *tiger!* Mrs. Floogle had to admit Mr. Floogle had been clever to know a bargain when he saw one.

But Amos said he was sure people facing tigers had to have much more than whips. So he found a picture.

Mrs. Floogle took one quick look at the picture and hurried off to oil and polish Big Grandfather's grandfather's gun, which Big Grandfather had kindly lent them to hang in the empty spot over the fireplace.

And Amos got his tools to saw part of the legs off a kitchen chair so that it would be handy to use, just in case Mr. Floogle or the tiger should need it.

But Fanny Flora braided her hair neatly and brushed her teeth properly and went to bed to dream of her wonderful, delightful, cozy kitten.

"With stripes, I hope," decided Fanny Flora. "I *do* like a kitten with stripes."

Next morning came, and oh! Mr. Floogle was a brave sight as he waited at the station for the train. There could be a train full of tigers—Mr. Floogle was ready. His whip curled carelessly around his shoulder. The sawed-off kitchen chair was in his right hand and Big Grandfather's grandfather's gun gleamed at his side.

But the train was late, and Mr. Floogle grew hot and tired. The gun was heavy, and the whip made his neck itch. So Mr. Floogle sat on the sawed-off chair and wished that Mrs. Floogle and Amos and Fanny Flora had not been *quite* so obedient when he told them sternly they must stay home. Being brave alone is lonely.

At last the train whistled down the track and sighed to a stop in front of the station. The door of the baggage car slid back, and Mr. Floogle was ready.

But nothing came out except the baggage-man's cheerful face.

"Two crates!" he shouted. "Get 'em off. Quick! The train's going to start again."

So there was nothing for Mr. Floogle to do but put down the whip and the gun and the chair and help the baggageman with the crates.

"This is Fanny Flora's kitten," said Mr. Floogle as he peeked in the first crate. "Striped. She wanted a striped kitten."

"Yep," said the baggageman, and they put the crate in the back of the Zoo truck.

"And this must be the tiger," said Mr. Floogle. But he was careful not to peek between the bars of *that* crate. Somehow, Mr. Floogle did not feel like looking into a tiger's green and gleaming eyes. Not even a baby tiger's green and gleaming eyes.

"Yep," said the baggageman. They put that crate in the back of the Zoo truck.

"Good-by!" The baggageman waved as the train snorted off and left Mr. Floogle alone with the Zoo's tiger and Fanny Flora's kitten.

"Well, good-by," said Mr. Floogle, and he climbed into the truck nervously. But he kept his foot on the chair, and the gun and the whip handy on the seat beside him. And he whistled loudly and bravely.

"I'll drive home first with Fanny Flora's kitten," decided Mr. Floogle. "Mrs. Floogle and Amos and Fanny Flora and *everyone* will see that tigers mean nothing to me." So he drove home, whistling louder and faster every time the truck bounced over a bump.

"Here's your kitten," called Mr. Floogle, and he carried the crate into the kitchen.

"Oh, oh!" Fanny Flora peeked into the crate.

"A striped kitten! *Just* what I wanted. Oh, the darling dear!"

Amos obligingly ran for the hammer, and Mr. Floogle pried open the crate, and Mrs. Floogle poured a saucer of milk. The kitchen was a loving, cheerful place for a new kitten.

"There we are," said Mr. Floogle when the last bar was off.

The kitten strolled out, every black stripe gleaming.

"Such sparkling green eyes!" said Amos admiringly.

"Such a handsome big head!" said Fanny Flora admiringly.

"And such a fine tail!" said Mrs. Floogle admiringly.

"A very *substantial* kitten," agreed Mr. Floogle.

But Snitkin said nothing at all. He dashed under the kitchen table and would NOT come out—not in any circumstances.

"Jealous," whispered Mr. Floogle. The other Floogles nodded their heads wisely and were quite disappointed in Snitkin.

"Where is the tiger?" asked Mrs. Floogle.

"In the truck," said Mr. Floogle calmly. "I must cart him along to the Zoo."

"We'll go, too," said Mrs. Floogle. "I've always wanted to see a tiger."

Mr. Floogle pretended.

Mr. Floogle scowled.

Mr. Floogle said it was dangerous.

But in his heart Mr. Floogle was glad. It is better to have company when you are being brave.

So they gave Fanny Flora's kitten a comfortable box with a pillow, and they all got into the truck and rode to the Zoo.

Then Mr. Floogle put on his leather gloves and carried the crate inside the Zoo.

Mrs. Floogle carried the whip.

Amos carried the gun.

Fanny Flora carried the chair.

"Our baby tiger!" said the Zoo Man happily, between sneezes. And he carefully opened the crate.

The whip was ready.

The chair was ready.

The gun was ready.

The Floogles were ready.

And out came the tiger—so little, so soft, so frightened!

"Ho, he'll have to do a lot of growing," said Mr. Floogle.

"A great lot of growing," agreed Mrs. Floogle, looking at the big tigers in the next cage.

Amos put away the whip and the chair and the gun.

"It is very odd," said the Zoo Man, and he looked puzzled all over his face.

"You should see our kitten," said Fanny Flora. "Much bigger. Much prouder. Much wider in the stripes."

And the Floogles went home to play with their kitten.

"You get very tired playing with one of Little Grandmother's kittens," sighed Fanny Flora at suppertime.

The kitten was tired, too. And hungry.

He drank all his milk. He drank all of Snitkin's milk.

He ate all his supper. He ate all of Snitkin's supper. He jumped up on the table and ate all the Floogles' supper.

"Well, really!" said Mrs. Floogle.

And the kitten growled deep, deep, and the fur on his throat danced with his growling.

The kitten was tired, and he slept. Not in the box with the pillow. Not behind the stove. Not on the floor. Right in the middle of Mr. Floogle's own comfortable chair.

"Scat!" said Mr. Floogle when he was ready to sit in his own comfortable chair and read the evening paper.

The kitten opened one green eye and growled.

Mr. Floogle read his evening paper in the kitchen.

Snitkin still would *not* come out from under the kitchen table—not in *any* circumstances. Mrs. Floogle and Amos and Fanny Flora tiptoed about, so as not to disturb their kitten. Mr.

Floogle turned the pages of his newspaper very quietly.

"I didn't know," sighed Mrs. Floogle, "that a kitten had such a *big* appetite."

"I didn't know," said Fanny Flora, "that a kitten had such a *big* growl."

"Poor Little Grandmother!" said Amos. "With a house full of kittens."

Just then someone knocked on the back door. In came the Zoo Man.

"I have been thinking," said the Zoo Man. "I have been thinking about my tiger. I have been thinking about your kitten."

Mr. Floogle looked at the Zoo Man. Mr. Floogle looked at Mrs. Floogle and Amos and Fanny Flora.

"Oh, my!" said Mr. Floogle. "Have you been thinking what I am thinking now?"

The Zoo Man nodded.

"What did the tag on the crate say?" he asked.

Mr. Floogle hung his head down, as though he was looking for crumbs on his vest.

Mr. Floogle's face turned red, as though he was looking at a hot fire.

Mr. Floogle whispered, "I forgot to wear my glasses. So I didn't look."

"Let's look now," said Mrs. Floogle.

So they looked at the tag on the crate. They looked at the kitten in Mr. Floogle's own comfortable chair. They looked at one another. And they laughed and they laughed and they laughed.

"Oh, my!" laughed Fanny Flora. "We've been playing with a tiger kitten!"

"And feeding a tiger kitten!" laughed Mrs. Floogle.

"And hearing a tiger kitten growl!" laughed Mr. Floogle.

"No wonder Snitkin would not come out!" laughed Amos.

Then the Zoo Man put on his leather gloves, and Mr. Floogle put on *his* leather gloves. And they carefully lifted the baby tiger into the crate.

They carried the crate to the Zoo Man's truck. When they came back to the kitchen, the Zoo Man had a lump under his coat.

"Here is my tiger," he said to Fanny Flora. And he reached inside his coat and brought out his tiger—so little, so soft, so full of purring, so cozy.

"Much better," said Mr. Floogle wisely.

"Much, much better," said Mrs. Floogle. And she began getting supper all over again for the kitten and Snitkin and the Floogles and the Zoo Man. And a spoonful of cherry cough medicine for the Zoo Man, too.

"Much, much, *much* better," Snitkin decided. He came out from under the kitchen table, his tail full of wagging and his heart full of love for the cuddly small kitten Little Grandmother had sent.

"Next time," said Mr. Floogle as he invited the Zoo Man to sit in his own comfortable chair, "next time I pick up a tiger, I will not worry about my leather gloves and my whip and my chair and Big Grandfather's grandfather's gun. But I *will* remember to carry my glasses in my left coat pocket."

And before supper the Zoo Man promised he'd never, *never*, *NEVER* tell even one of the neighbors about the *extremely substantial* kitten who'd spent the day with the Floogles.

10: The Floogles Give a Party

The Floogles decided to give a party.
"And high time we did," Mr. Floogle said.
"All the parties there are in the world, and none of them ours."

So the Floogles agreed to have a splendid party. Not big. But fancy. Really fancy.

Mr. Floogle wrote down the names of the people he wanted to invite.

Mrs. Floogle wrote down the names of the people she wanted to invite.

Amos wrote down names.

Fanny Flora wrote down names.

Even Snitkin had a few friends who would gladly wait around the kitchen for a sandwich.

When the names were written down the Floogles put them all together on one list. And oh, my! The list was as long as the kitchen table.

"Dear me! This will not do!" cried Mrs. Floogle. "All these people! We must cross out some names."

But the Floogles could not and would not.

Cross out Fifth Cousin Jasper? Oh, no!

Cross out Cousin Oscar? Oh, no!

Cross out Aunt Hepzibah? Oh, no!

Little Grandmother? Big Grandfather? No! The teacher? Oh, no!

The Zoo Man? The Sheriff, perhaps? The Mayor? The Governor? No, no, no!

"What shall we do?" asked poor, puzzled Mrs. Floogle. "We can never get so many people in our house."

"Very simple," said Amos. "We'll make the house bigger."

"Who wants a bigger house?" said Fanny

Flora. "Just that much more to dust. Just that much more to sweep and to scrub."

"What we need," said Mr. Floogle wisely, "is a bigger house for a party and a same-size house for a cleaning." So Mr. Floogle and Amos went off to think it over.

Before night came Amos and Mr. Floogle had everything nicely worked out.

They measured and hammered and nailed until they had two fine walls.

They sawed and they sawed until they had the front wall of the house neatly cut off.

They hammered and hammered until they had the front wall nailed to the new side walls.

Then they pushed and they *pushed* and they PUSHED until the new walls slipped inside the old walls and the front wall fitted snugly.

"There!" said Mr. Floogle. "When the party comes, we push on the front wall and out it slides to make a party-sized house."

"When the party goes, we push the front wall

in again to make our own-sized house," explained Amos proudly.

"Just like a dresser drawer," said Fanny Flora.

"Exactly," said Mr. Floogle, and he sat down in his own comfortable chair for a rest.

How happy the Floogles were! Amos and Fanny Flora wrote the invitations and didn't cross out a single name.

Mrs. Floogle was so pleased that she made chocolate pie for supper, with bananas sliced prettily over the top.

Mr. Floogle, who was a little tired—and no wonder—took a small nap in his own comfortable chair. The harder Mr. Floogle slept, the harder Mr. Floogle breathed. Puff in, puff out, puff in, puff out. Harder, harder, harder.

In the middle of a puff, Mrs. Floogle came to the living room to boast a small boast about the pretty chocolate pie. But instead, she screamed a small scream. For as Mr. Floogle breathed out and breathed in, the front wall slid out and slid in, slid out and slid in.

"Oh, dear!" said Mrs. Floogle. "I can never stand this. A house that slides in and slides out is sure to make me nervous. A house that's bigger and smaller when someone breathes is very *confusing*."

She woke up Mr. Floogle, and he obligingly rummaged through his tool chest until he found two large safety pins.

"Tomorrow I will buy hooks," he promised.

So Mrs. Floogle went on getting the supper, and Amos and Fanny Flora went on writing the invitations, and Mr. Floogle went on sitting in his own comfortable chair. But everyone was quite careful about breathing in the living room. Especially toward the front wall.

Early the next morning Mr. Floogle hurried to the hardware store and bought four of the largest hooks. On the way home, he mailed the invitations to the party.

Mrs. Floogle and Amos and Fanny Flora kindly breathed out so as to push the front wall out a bit. This made everything handier for **Mr.** Floogle while he was screwing in the hooks.

"There," he said at last.

Then Mrs. Floogle and Amos and Fanny Flora breathed in to bring the front wall tight.

The hooks held the walls snug, no matter how hard anybody breathed. Mr. Floogle was quite pleased with himself and his work.

But Mrs. Floogle, who had been thinking unusually hard, said, "This is going to be very awkward at the party. Our house is larger, but our floor is not. It will be *very* awkward."

The Floogles unhooked the hooks.

The Floogles breathed the walls out.

The Floogles looked.

It was true. The floor went so far—and then nothing, nothing but the ground 'way down.

Snitkin found the arrangement pleasant and handy. He buried his second-best bone in a convenient spot. But the Floogles shook their heads in despair.

"Everybody is doing the polka," said Amos, "and bang-bang-bang! They fall off the floor."

"Big Grandfather and Little Grandmother are leading the Grand March," said Mrs. Floogle, "and suddenly they are gone."

"Cousin Oscar is waltzing with me," said Fanny Flora, "and all at once we must waltz in the air."

"Something must be done," said Mrs. Floogle wisely.

"We have walls that slide," said Amos. "Now we need a floor that slides, too."

"Of course," said Mr. Floogle.

So Mr. Floogle and Amos measured and sawed and hammered and nailed. And before too long they had a floor. They nailed the new walls to the new floor.

"Just a matter of careful planning," said Mr.

Floogle wisely as they pushed the new walls *and* the new floor.

"Be a little careful pushing, please!" cried Mrs. Floogle.

For the new floor was pushing *everything,* and the chairs and the tables and the company sofa were flying out the back door faster than Mrs. Floogle and Fanny Flora could catch them.

But at last everything was straightened up.

The Floogles carried in the tables and the chairs and the company sofa and arranged them neatly on top of the new floor.

Mr. Floogle fastened the hooks. Then, being a little tired—and no wonder—he sat down in his own comfortable chair to wait for supper.

"Odd!" said Mr. Floogle. "My comfortable chair has always been extremely comfortable. And now it is extremely *un*comfortable."

So he got up to look. It didn't need much looking to find the trouble. Two legs of Mr. Floogle's comfortable chair were on the edge of the new floor. Two legs were on the old floor. And Mr. Floogle's comfortable chair was going *teeter, teeter, teeter.*

Mr. Floogle wisely moved his chair and said nothing about the matter. But before bedtime the rest of the Floogles found that little step-up.

Fanny Flora stubbed her toe so hard that she feared she would not be able to waltz.

Amos tripped while he was carrying a full bowl of fresh, hot, buttered popcorn. So the Floogles got none of it. Except Snitkin. And he got a stomach-ache.

And poor Mrs. Floogle did nothing but fall up and fall down the little step. Before the evening was over the Floogles had broken fourteen plates, two cups, three saucers and a dish nobody had ever liked anyway. They were all *very* annoyed and unhappy and angry and full of aching toes. Except Snitkin, and he, of course, was full of stomach-aches.

"No party!" said Mr. Floogle, and he marched off to bed.

"No party!" said Mrs. Floogle, and she tried to fit the fourteen plates together for gluing.

"No party?" cried Fanny Flora.

"Tomorrow is another day," said Amos wisely. And he went to bed to think.

Next day was the day of the party, even if there wasn't going to be one. The mailman came early and the mailman came often, bringing letters to the Floogles. Letters from Big Grandfather and Little Grandmother and Aunt Hepzibah and Fifth Cousin Jasper and Mr. Floogle's Cousin Oscar and the teacher and everyone.

"We're coming to your party," said the letters.

"Oh, my!" said Mrs. Floogle. "They're all coming."

"Oh, me!" said Mr. Floogle. "We're having a party whether we want to or not."

"We *must* THINK," said Amos and Fanny Flora. So the Floogles limped around, thinking.

Mrs. Floogle made four cakes, while they thought.

Fanny Flora made chocolate frosting, while they thought.

Amos cracked walnuts, while they thought.

Mr. Floogle turned the handle on the ice-cream freezer, while they thought.

"It's a beautiful day," said Mr. Floogle. "It will be a beautiful night."

"A warm night, with just a whisper of breeze to rustle the leaves," said Mrs. Floogle.

"And a deep-blue sky full of stars to wish on," said Fanny Flora.

"No need at all to be behind lace curtains," said Amos.

"No need for a roof," said Mr. Floogle.

"No need for walls," said Mrs. Floogle.

"But plenty of need for a floor," said Fanny Flora. "For the waltz."

"For the polka," said Mrs. Floogle.

"For the Grand March," said Amos.

"Why are we waiting?" asked Mr. Floogle.

And then how the Floogles hurried!

They unhooked the hooks.

They breathed out hard.

They unnailed the new floor.

They unnailed the new walls.

They laid the new floor in the nicest part of the yard.

They made the new walls into new floors and laid them in the nicest part of the yard, too.

They hung paper lanterns on the trees.

They carried out the table for the cakes.

They brought out the company sofa for Big Grandfather and Little Grandmother.

Then they nailed the front wall back on the house and pasted the cracks with the finest flour-and-water paste Mrs. Floogle could stir up.

When the guests came to the party there were the paper lanterns glowing brighter than the fireflies, and the cakes glistening in their chocolate frosting, and fifty-two million stars to wish

158

on, and the fiddler all tuned up with a handkerchief under his chin to fiddle for the waltzing.

Everyone was invited, and everyone was there. The Zoo Man came early. *Without* his tiger. The Mayor was splendid in his silk hat, and the Governor wore a red ribbon to prove he was Governor. Fanny Flora looked fetching in blue hair ribbons that just matched the blue bow Little Grandmother brought for her kitten.

And as the party was getting well started, with all the ladies looking pretty and all the gentlemen handsome, who should come wandering in but the old photographer!

"Just in time for the party," said Mr. Floogle happily.

"Just in time for a picture," said the old photographer, with never a word about the Floogles standing on their heads.

It was a wonderful party! And no one even *dreamed* that the Floogles had had a confusing time of it. Of course, the Floogles couldn't help a small limp now and then. But the party guests thought this a new and very clever way of waltzing. Before the evening was over everyone was limp-waltzing too, right along with the Floogles. If they hadn't been giving the party, Mr. Floogle and Mrs. Floogle would surely have won the waltzing prize. As it was the Sheriff, who was the best good-waltzing judge in the state, decided Cousin Oscar and Aunt Hepzibah won.

The Floogles didn't mind a bit. For as Mr. Floogle said, "It wouldn't have been fair to win. After all, think of all the extra practice we had, falling up and falling down from the old floor to the new floor, and from the new floor to the old floor."

So after the party the Floogles blew out all the paper lanterns, ate the last bit of chocolate frosting, wished on the fifty-two million stars and went happily to bed.